T0198770

Everything is Everything
Finding Your Magic

Sally Kingman

Balboa Press books may be ordered through booksellers or by contacting:

Balboa Press
A Division of Hay House
1663 Liberty Drive
Bloomington, IN 47403
www.balboapress.com
844-682-1282

ISBN: 978-1-9822-7598-3 (sc)
978-1-9822-7599-0 (e)

Library of Congress Control Number: 2021921445

Print information available on the last page.

Balboa Press rev. date: 11/11/2021

BALBOA.PRESS
A DIVISION OF HAY HOUSE

Everything is Everything
Finding Your Magic

Once upon a time, in a magical land, Sally said, "No." Here is how it happened.

It was a sun kissed morning, the Spring air filled with the aroma of wildflowers and fresh new earth, bees were buzzing all around just as the butterflies were drifting on the air currents warmed by the luxurious late morning rays.

The grass in the meadow was deep and thick, dense with the energy of new life, "this must be what Heaven smells like," Sally said to Pup.

She had been lost in thought for some time, cocooned in this world of new, this scent of hope and possibility. These early morning hours were her favorite, wandering aimlessly amongst her friends, the flowers, the trees, the plants, the animals. This is where her cup was filled up. Her little pup joyfully trotting beside her, until he zipped off to chase a newly spied butterfly or bumblebee always ready for an adventure

And then the voice, did she really hear it? Or had she heard it so often that she was somehow hearing it from her own mind? "Stop, come in now, it is time to get to work, we have things to do. How many times have I told you that you live in a fanciful world of butterfies and talking trees? There is no value to these hours you spend dancing around in the meadow. How many times can you stare at a blade of grass?"

Today, however, before answering, before blindly jumping up and following the voice, she took a breath, and then another, and then another. She noticed her heart beat seeming to strengthen, the sky was filling with birds she had not even noticed before, hawks, eagles, bluebirds, great blue herons, hummingbirds, they all were flying above her; it was as if they were sending her their strength. Her canine companion ran around her barking and barking as if to add his vitality to all that was building around and within his beloved girl.

Sally felt a sense of power and self-determination welling up from within which she did not ever remember feeling; from deep within her throat, coming from the bottom of her belly she heard herself, say **NO**, then **NO, NO, NO**. I do not have to listen to this voice, I do not need to leave this place of happiness.

"There is value to dancing around in the meadow!!! I no longer will listen to that voice calling me away from what I love. Everything is a part of everything. Who I am and what makes me happy counts!! I am just as much a part of the glorious Beauty of the meadow as are the butterfies and the trees."

Sally closed her eyes to envelop herself in the sensation of this moment, when she opened them it was as if the world had taken on a technicolor glow!!! She began to look around with what seemed like new eyes, colors were brighter, the sun's glow reflected on everything as it must have on that first morning of Creation itself; she heard the music of the trees more profoundly than ever. As she turned around with a dumbfounded gaze she saw things in her beloved meadow which she had never noticed; paths leading off out of the meadow in all directions. Which one to take? Where to go first? Just pick one, her heart told her so off she went followed by her faithful companion who was ALWAYS up for fun.

The inviting path was soft underfoot with wild geranium, spring beauty, bloodroot and all manner of Spring flowers surrounding it. Sally almost held her breath as she walked on, there was such a feeling of Peace and Reverence infusing the air. Once again she felt herself breath deeply, she could feel her feet fall sweetly upon this path each step grounding her into a sense of herself. She took a rest on a log beside the path, when out of the corner of her eye she spied a small fairy-like woodland person who skipped over and sat right down next to her on the log!!! Pup came over and sat down right in front of the odd couple curious as to what might happen now.

In the sweetest little lilting voice this curious new friend greeted Sally, and her pup, with a cheery, "Howdy-do? How are you two today? What's up and welcome, welcome, welcome. Tell me what's been happening this beautiful Spring morning."

Pup's tail wagged in the grass sending bits of leaves and flower petals flying in all directions. Sally took a breath, to steady herself in the presence of this odd little person and returned the greeting, "Good morning yourself. We are very well thank you,simply enjoying this beautiful day. My name is Sally and this is Pup. What is your name?"

"Crystal-Claire, thank you, and I am happy to see you simply enjoying the day. Tell me, how did you find yourself in this place?"

Before she could respond further Sally took a moment to take in everything about her surprizing companion. Crystal-Claire was simply the most endearing, comforting, enchanting being Sally had ever encountered. Her appearance was whimsical, her clothes all mixed-up bright colors, colors her own mother would never had paired in an outfit, while her glistening hair curled out in all directions. Her golden eyes sparkeled. There was a delightful scent which seemed to eminate from Crystal-Claire along with a comforting presence which made Sally feel as if they had known each other forever.

"Well, I suppose I'd have to say by surprise. You see, Pup and I were doing what we normally do on a lovely morning as this, lolly-gagging around in the meadow listening to the birds, chasing butterflies, memorizing each beautiful blade of grass. Do you realize that each blade has it's very own telltale markings, lines, shades of green, creases, tears, and holes? It is as if each blade has it's own fingerprint, unique and special; Pup and I actually can tell blades apart, we look for our favorites each time we are able to visit the meadow. We love each one for its own beauty but then when we look at the whole meadow, as we sit still or run around, we can not help but be dazzled by the magic of the Whole meadow; can you see that? How each blade is a perfectly beautiful creation of its own then when looked at a part of a whole, the Perfection and Beauty compounds to something almost too beautiful to be explained in words? I was lost in the wonder of this when I was interrupted by the Voice."

"The Voice," Crystal-Claire queried with a puzzled look on her face. "What is the Voice?"

"Ugh, you don't want to know, trust me. It is a voice, I think I first actually heard it from a real person, or maybe even a lot of people. Maybe it was someone in my family, or a teacher, or Sunday school teacher, maybe it was the voice of a character in a book....I read a lot of books. Wherever it came from, I think it is now stuck in my head."

Crystal-Claire seemed to listen to Sally with her whole body, so intent was her concentration. She intuited this to be a very important conversation, "What does this Voice say to you?"

"Mostly it tells me to stop, especially if I am not doing anything which could be called productive. It keeps me in line, it's like being told to stay in the lines when coloring in a coloring book. Use the right colors, don't be messy, don't do anything weird or frivalous. It makes me feel unimportant and worthless, as if I was not enough just being me, that I am valued only by what I do not by who I am. Do you understand me, Crystal-Claire?"

"Yes, I hear what you are saying and it makes me sad. It would be like telling one of your beautiful blades of grass that it has no place in the meadow. That it doesn't fit in the picture. Tell me, how did you get here?"

"WELL, today for some reason, when I heard the voice, I said NO, NO, NO, NO!" I told myself I was important, I didn't need to stop and listen to that voice any more. And then, the world changed for me, it was as if I opened my eyes for the first time. I saw the path which led me to your meadow and I followed it!!!! Here we are."

Crystal-Claire almost could not contain her happiness at hearing Sally's reponse, she jumped off the log and actually danced with joy, Pup joining in with his own yips, yaps, howls and licks. "You've found it, you've found it, the magic of Life!!! From now on each day will be better and better than the day before, Sally! You have chosen YOURSELF. This is a wonderful day indeed," Sally's new friend exclaimed.

Crystal-Claire went on to tell Sally, and of course Pup as he was sitting transfixed by this magical little person, "Sally, so you see all of these paths leading off in different directions?"

"Yes, I do," Sally responded, "each one looks so inviting, they are different aren't they? I get the feeling that each one leads off into something unique and exciting. What can you tell me about them, Crystal-Claire?"

"Each path leads to a new adventure! New people, places, things. There are adventures awaiting you on these paths which exceed your wildest imagination. Now that you have said NO to that nasty old Voice you have rediscovered your own power to see the paths. You now have the freedom of choice to take which ever path you feel like taking whenever you feel like taking it. **Ta-da**, *icing on the cake*, now, you have eyes to see, ears to hear, and a heart to listen to ALL of the Heavenly beings lighting your path!!! You don't think it is simply a coincidence that I chose this log, in this meadow, at this time to sit and take a rest, do you?"

Sally could only sit and stare at her new found friend. Could this really be true? Do all of these exciting new adventures truly lie ahead? Sitting at her feet, Pup gently laid his head on her knee as if to reassure her that, yes, this is real.

A feeling welled up in her heart so strongly that Sally did indeed believe. She knew because the belief came from her heart not her head. Placing her hand on her beloved pup's soft sweet head, she took a deep breath as her countenance reflected her new found self-love.

Crystal-Claire waited patiently as her companion took this all in, as the smile broke out on Sally's face, Crystal-Claire spoke up, "my dear, I see that you understand, well done, welcome home. I think for today this is enough, you have done a great deal of work to come this far, you are at the door of a brand new way of living but there is no need to rush. Come here to the meadow any time you wish, pick a path. I will be here to walk with you if you would like, just call my name or even just think of me and I will be with you."

Sally had looked away for one second to check on Pup, when she glanced back to the log Crystal-Claire was no longer there. What? Had she really been there? Was she dreaming this, had she fallen asleep? As she looked around more closely Sally found a small blue feather where Crystal-Claire had been sitting; she knew, yes, this peculiar little person had been there.

Sally picked up the feather, stood up so that she and Pup could leave the meadow for today. She knew she would be back, she was excited to pick a path, to have a new adventure and she knew in her heart Crystal-Claire and Pup would be right there with her.

Printed in the United States
by Baker & Taylor Publisher Services